What's the Weather?

IT'S RAINy!

By Alex Appleby

 Gareth Stevens
Publishing

Please visit our website, www.garethstevens.com. For a free color catalog of all our
high-quality books, call toll free 1-800-542-2595 or fax 1-877-542-2596.

Library of Congress Cataloging-in-Publication Data

Appleby, Alex.
It's Rainy! / by Alex Appleby.
   p. cm. — (What's the weather)
Includes index.
ISBN 978-1-4339-9397-8 (pbk.)
ISBN 978-1-4339-9398-5 (6-pack)
ISBN 978-1-4339-9396-1 (library binding)
1. Rain and rainfall — Juvenile literature. 2. Weather — Juvenile literature. I. Appleby, Alex. II. Title.
QC924.7 A66 2014
551.577—dc23

First Edition

Published in 2014 by
Gareth Stevens Publishing
111 East 14th Street, Suite 349
New York, NY 10003

Copyright © 2014 Gareth Stevens Publishing

Editor: Ryan Nagelhout
Designer: Andrea Davison-Bartolotta

All illustration by Michael Harmon

Printed in the United States of America

CPSIA compliance information: Batch #CS13GS: For further information contact Gareth Stevens, New York, New York at 1-800-542-2595.

Contents

It is raining!

The sky is full of clouds.

Rain falls
from the clouds.

I go out in the rain.

I wear a
yellow raincoat.

Big pink boots keep my feet dry.

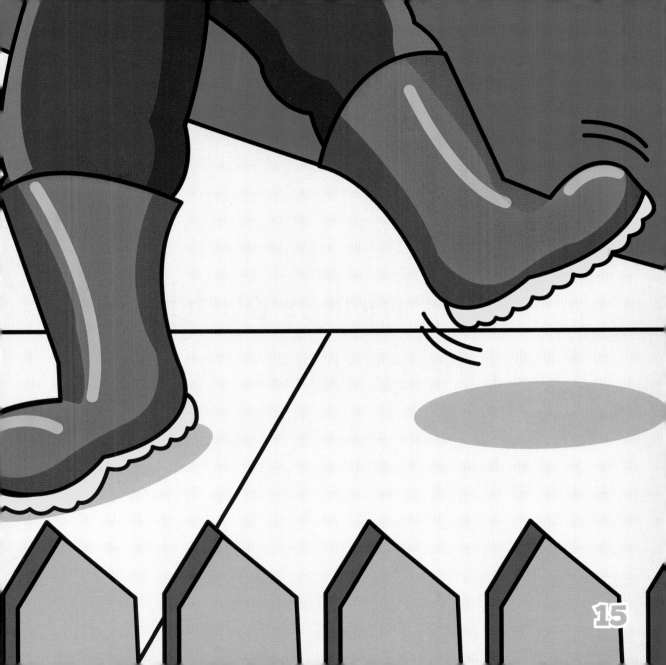

15

Water makes puddles on the ground.

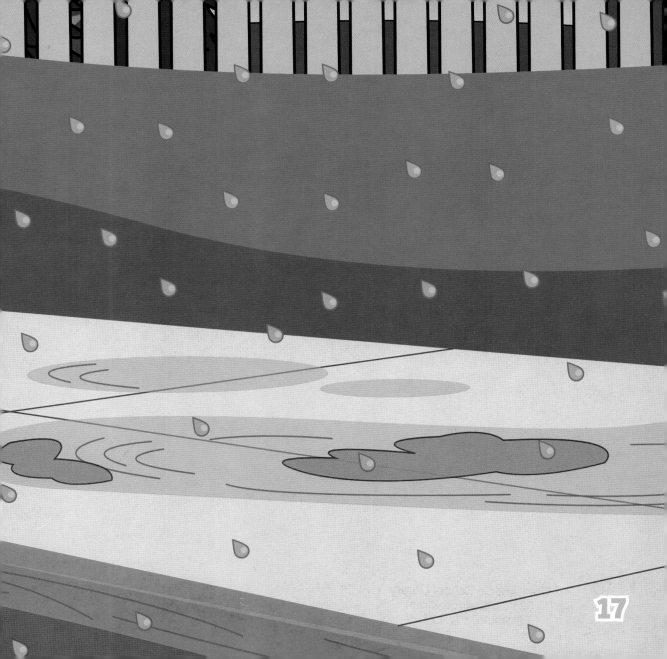

17

I jump in them with my boots. They get covered in mud!

19

Rain helps
my roses grow.

The rain fills a blue barrel. My mom uses it to water her roses.

23

Words to Know

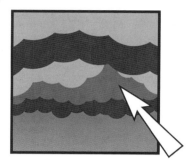

clouds

raincoat

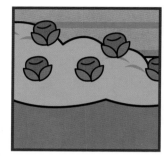

roses

Index